LENNIE GRACE

101 Horror Drabbles

Bite Sized Horrors #3

First edition

This book was professionally typeset on Reedsy.
Find out more at reedsy.com

Contents

II The Horrible Humans

I

The Mean Monsters

1

The Monster Moves

Melissa watched the monster that killed her mother creep out of the kitchen and down the hall. The front door rattled and whined as it opened. Then it slammed shut with a BANG!

Melissa rushed to the living room window and peeked out through the crack in the curtains.

The monster's horrible, glowing smirk lit up a patch of darkness around it as it crossed the empty street. Slowly, in crept to the neighbor's lawn and slunk low against the ground. It squirmed its way through a crack in the wall and into the neighbor's basement. The monster's new home.

2

The Sleeping Cage

I never understood why my parents forced my brother to sleep in a cage in the basement.

They said it was to protect him. To protect us. I didn't believe them. I hated that cage.

It was abuse!

One night, I snuck down to let him loose. He slept peacefully.

Until I unlocked the cage.

He lept out, knocking me to the floor. His eyes were wrong.

Evil.

Then the rest of him changed.

This was my brother.

But at the same time... not.

My brother didn't have fangs, claws, or scales.

Maybe the cage wasn't so bad after all.

3

The Last Egg

For our science fair project, my friends and I hatched chicken eggs. It was fun, and going really well.

They started hatching.

We watched as one by one, the eggs broke open. Tiny yellow chicks covered in eggy goop struggled to freedom.

So cute!

So tiny!

So helpless.

Soon there was only one egg left.

As cracks formed on the shell, the chicks peeped loudly.

Crack!

The last egg burst apart. And dragon a rushed towards our chickens.

That's right.

A dragon.

It roared a tiny roar as it attacked our chickens, filling the room with terrified peeps.

And blood.

4

The Auction

She struggled as they dragged her on stage. She cried for help, but no one moved. In fact, most of the audience laughed.

Maybe we should have felt bad for her, this young woman crying and trembling with terror. We would've once upon a time. Back when we were human.

But that was just it.

We *weren't* human.

Not anymore.

I licked my lips. My tongue scraped against my fangs as I smelled her blood.

Then the bidding started.

"One thousand!"

"Two thousand!"

"Three thousand!"

"Five thousand!" I shouted, determined to win her. She smelled delicious. And I was thirsty.

5

The Thing at the End of the Rainbow

It was supposed to be a Leprechaun.

Everyone knew that. You followed the rainbow until you found its end. When you did, you got to keep the pot of gold.

If you could kill the monster guarding it, obviously.

It should've been easy.

A cute little guy in a green outfit. That was what the stories said.

Just one quick, clean shot, and I'd be rich. That was the plan.

it was supposed to be a leprechaun.

Not a troll.

A *troll* the size of a building with a club to match.

Needless to say, I didn't get the gold.

6

The Dreams

Ever since I threw that penny down the well, everything I dream comes true.

Last week, I dreamed I had a sports car. I found one in the garage the next morning. Then I dreamed I could invisible whenever I want to. That's an awesome power.

Then I dreamed I met my favorite celebrity. I ran into them the next day.

It's been a good week.

Too good.

Guess the universe had to balance it out.

Yesterday, I dreamed I was kidnapped by devilish monsters. I'm scared to leave my house. Because I know I won't be coming back alive.

7

The Coffee Thing

She shuffled into the kitchen, her foggy mind focused on one thing, and one thing only.

Coffee.

She set up the machine and turned it on. Then she turned it on and leaned against the table to watch it brew.

Drip.

Drip.

Drip.

Watching it fill the pot was so hypnotic, she didn't realize something was wrong until it was too late.

An arm made of sludgy brown grounds creeped out of the top of the coffee maker. It flopped on the counter and started growing.

Growing.

Growing.

Until it was big enough to wrap its fingers around her throat.

8

The Monster and the Stepmom

"Let me out! I'll tell Dad!"

Judy laughed. "Go ahead. He won't believe you."

I cried. She was right.

"Please! I'm sorry! Don't leave me here!"

"You're staying put."

Her footsteps headed downstairs, towards the living room. I was alone.

But not for long.

I huddled against the door. Waiting.

A minute later, it came.

The vent monster.

Slimy, bloody tentacles rose from the air vent and flopped on the carpet. It hated when the door was locked. The tentacles crawled towards me.

I cried but didn't move. Why bother? She locked the door.

And there was nowhere to run.

9

Playing With My Hair

Something tugged my braid as I worked at my computer. I smiled but didn't turn around. My kitten loved climbing on the back of my chair and watching me type. She also loved playing with my braid.

It was only a little distracting, so I let her stay.

"Hi, kitty bean," I chuckled. "Did you need some company?"

"No…" a strange voice hissed.

My fingers went still and ridged on the keyboard. I lived alone. So who -or *what*- was behind me?

"I'm… hungry…"

"W-what do you w-want?" I whimpered.

"Your… Hair…"

I screamed as claws dug into my skull.

10

In Bed With Me

I smiled sleepily as the bed shifted under my husband's weight. A blast of cold air hit my naked skin as he lifted the comforter and crawled in next to me.

"Mmm," I mumbled and snuggled closer. "How was work?"

He didn't answer. I assumed that meant it wasn't a good day.

Ding!

Tiredly, I reached for my phone. My blood ran cold as I read my husband's text.

Hey, babe. Stuck working extra tonight. Be home real late. Love you!

If he was at work… Who… Or What was in bed with me? I was too scared to look.

11

My Zombie Daughter

She stands in the corner of the basement, growling softly.

She stinks. Her arm is gone. Maggots squirm across her rotting flesh. Strong chains hold her in the corner, but I know she'll try to devour me if she ever gets loose.

I know I shouldn't keep her. The other survivors would be so furious if they ever found out. A zombie in our midst? They'd happily use one of our last bullets on me.

But what else can I do? She's my daughter. My last family member. And zombie or not, I swore I'd always be there for her.

12

Giants and Farms

The world ended. Not with aliens, bombs, or Jesus coming back.

But with giants.

You know, the ones from the storybooks?

Yeah.

Those kinds.

They did the sorts of things you'd expect from humongous monsters. They smashed bridges, pushed over buildings. Crushes terrified people under stinking feet.

Then they took over, rearranging our world for their needs. Their first order of business?

Round us up and put us in farms.

That's right, they turned us into farm animals. Like cows or goats.

Except we don't get to go to the slaughterhouse. They like to eat us raw.

Bit.

By.

Bit.

13

The Blood Factory

Jessica trembled as the vampires stopped at her cage. They looked her over, consulting their files.

Jessica wanted to kill them all.

But she couldn't.

The vampires owned all the humans here. Fighting only made things worse.

"The test groups loved 1325B's blood," said the leader vampire. She tapped her pen against the cage bars. "We need more from it."

"We can't take any more blood. It's already giving the max amount."

"Any more and we'll kill it."

"True. But we *can* clone it."

"It'll be painful for it."

They all laughed at that.

"So?"

Then they dragged Jessica out.

14

Together

Together the things crawled through the darkness of the forest, dragging themselves towards the warm glow of the campfire.

The humans' camp looked so inviting. So full of warmth.

Of life.

Of food.

Slowly, they surrounded the campfire, lingering just outside the light.

The humans talked and laughed and ate, completely unaware of their danger.

Together, the things used the trees to pull themselves up. They towered almost as tall as the trees.

Together, they roared their hunger.

Together, the things stepped into the light.

The humans screamed.

Together, the things laughed.

Together, the things attacked.

Together, the things fed.

15

The Bigfoot Team

I laughed when my friends left on their expedition into the woods. They were looking for Bigfoot. How could I *not* laugh?

I laughed again when they came back, calling me and begging me to come to George's house.

"Get over here!" Wyatt begged. "You have to see what we found!"

I laughed the whole drive over. I expected blurry photos and samples of hair that would eventually turn out to belong to a moose or elk or whatever.

I didn't expect them to actually catch one. And I certainly didn't except them to bring it back in a cage.

16

What is it?

Two kids stand above me, staring curiously.

"What is it?" One asks.

"I don't know. A snake?"

"Snakes don't have long legs, dummy. It's some kinda lizard!"

I sigh.

What a know-it-all. Who lets kids go into the woods alone nowadays? Weren't all the parents scared of killer kidnapper or something?

"Maybe it's part scorpion. See the tail!"

"You think it's asleep?" the first kid asks.

I was trying to be.

"I don't know. Gimme that stick! Imma poke it!"

I open my eyes.

The first kid jabs me with the stick. I *wanted* to let them live.

Not anymore.

17

Invasion

It crawls up my spine, the tiny monster the doctors released into me. It'll help me walk again, they say.

I want that so badly. To walk again.

But not like this.

Not as part of their sick experiment. Not with an alien monster sharing my body.

Hello, host. A voice that isn't mine whispers in between my devastated thoughts.

"Get out!" I beg.

The doctors watch, but don't interfere. The alien monster makes itself more comfortable.

I like it here, it hums excitedly.

It helps me stand.

Then walk.

But I feel no joy. All I feel is invaded.

18

The Boring Old Statute

"Mom! I'm booooored!"

"We're not done looking at everything," Mom says. She tries to sound upbeat, but her tone and smile are wearing thin.

"But this is so lame!"

"It's art! It's good for you!"

I groan, but she keeps dragging me through the museum. Finally, she has to go to the bathroom. She leaves me alone to look at statues.

I sit on a bench and glare at a statue of a Minotaur. "You're the *most* boring," I grumble. I pull out my phone.

When I look up, the statue stands over me, swinging its sword down at me.

19

Mr. Carrots

Mr. Carrots.

My English teacher's pet. He came to school every day to hang out with us. A huge brown rabbit who loved nibbling on hay and posing for selfies with the students. I loved his twitchy nose.

I loved him.

Until he started torturing me.

Until I started hearing his sickly sweet voice in my head, telling me my worst fears.

I loved him less then.

Then he entered my dreams, showing me my fears and laughing as he hopped through blood.

My teacher loved the "creative stories" I wrote about Mr. Carrots.

They weren't stories.

They were warnings.

20

The zoo of magical creatures

When the magical creatures were discovered, zoos, aquariums, and theme parks were the first to profit.

Commercials aired day and night boasting real-life mermaids and kelpies! Feast your eyes on the great thunderbirds of North America. Be the first in your family to hold a dragon hatchling! See a manticore up close! Come to the sea monster feeding at six!

It was fun and games and wonder. Until the magical creatures began to fight back. They didn't like the cages and tanks. They wanted out. They wanted their freedom back. And they were writing their message in big blood-red letters.

21

The Trash Monster

It floated in the middle of the ocean. Growing bigger and bigger. Stronger and stronger. Until it wasn't just a heaping pile of endless waste floating it the Pacific.

It was a live.

It was strong.

And it wanted things.

It wanted to reach the land. To meet the humans who had created it. To say hello. And thank you for giving it life.

Slowly, it drew more and more garbage to it, getting even larger. Animals fled from it. Or they tried too. It was hard to flee an ocean filling with garbage when you couldn't walk on land.

22

Never Name It

It was sort of cute, this mutant creature they had created.

Two heads, one cat and one dog, sat on its shoulders. The body of a cute little corgi with the sweet toes of a kitty. A long fluffy kitty tail.

The scientists liked it, this strange thing. It purred, played fetch, and knew twenty different commands.

They called it Frankie.

They shouldn't have named it. That was one of the biggest rules of experimenting on animals.

Never name it.

Never love it

Never care.

Naming it only made it that much harder when they had to destroy Frankie.

23

The Broken Glass

Crack.

A long thing line appears in my glass prison.

Crack.

Then another one.

And another one.

And another.

Until at last, the glass in nothing but a big, complicated spiderweb of broken glass, just waiting to shatter.

Slowly, I reach out and tap the glass with one, long claw.

The glass falls, crashing to the floor with me and all the water in my tank. I flop to the concrete, grunting in pain until my tail becomes legs, and I can walk.

I rise unsteadily and go to kill my captors. They'd pay for treating me like an animal.

Regular Citizen

I'm not a monster. At least, not *all* the time.

I'm just a regular citizen.

I go to work five days a week. I'm rarely late or sick. I pay my bills and taxes. I keep my home tidy. Every week I meet with my book club at the local library. I volunteer at a local soup kitchen twice a month. I eat right and jog three times a week.

I like to think I'm a good member of the community.

Except when the moon is full. Then I… I can't control myself. I lose myself.

And the werewolf takes over.

25

When the Dragon Grew Up

It started out so small and cute, my dragon. I fed him bits of chicken and pork out of my hand. I taught him to fly. I taught him to catch mice and rats. I taught him how to swoop down and scare raccoons out of the garden.

It was all going so well.

Then he got too big to eat rodents anymore.

I tried to keep up with his hunger. I bought chicken by the truckload.

But it wasn't enough.

I hope the deer and elk keep him happy.

I hope he never finds out how good humans taste.

II

The Horrible Humans

26

Pictures to Delete

She doesn't *want* to get rid of them. She loves them. But she has to.

The police are starting to ask questions. If they find these… She'll be locked up.

One by one, she deletes the pictures. She feels awful as her collection goes away. Forever.

The man in the flowered shirt.

The old lady in the pantsuit.

The girl with the puffy scarf.

The boy in the grubby sweater.

The baby in the purple dinosaur onesie.

The pictures of her kills. Her accomplishments. They had to go.

She laughed when she killed them.

She cries when she deletes them.

27

My Ex-Best Friend

Most people have nice, happy collections of photos. Baby pictures. Cheesy family photos. Photos of their sunburned selves on cheap-ass vacations. Cute pet pictures.

Not me.

I'm different.

What's the saying? Oh yeah.

I'm not like other girls.

My photo albums are filled with pictures of all the people I've killed. I'm proud of them. Of course, I had to print them and put them in a pretty album.

I like the ones with lots of blood. Red. My favorite color.

But my vert favorite photo is of my first very victim. My first drowning. My best friend.

Ex-best friend.

28

Weekend Plans

It's Monday. And like every other teenager, I hate Mondays. No one likes coming back to school.

But i especially hate them because every Monday, my English teacher makes us write about what we did over the weekend.

I want to tell the truth. But I can't. She'd get me in big trouble if I write down that I spent the weekend following my ex and hiding under her bed.

So I lie.

I say I watched a movie when I actually watched Maya. I say I baked cookies when I really stole Maya's diary.

I lied. I had to.

29

Better Her Than Me

My sister's body looked small in the shallow hole I'd dug. Bruises covered her. Blood coated the back of her head.

"Better her than me," I muttered.

Trying not to cry, I placed her doll in her cold arms. So she'd have company on her trip to heaven.

I'd go to hell when Dad finally killed me.

My phone buzzed in my pocket. I pulled it out to check the text.

You done yet? he demands.

Almost.

Hurry. I'm hungry.

I sobbed quietly and start shoveling dirt over her. I felt so guilty. But I knew.

Better her than me.

30

Back to School Shopping

I stare in amazement at the huge selection of back-to-school stuff. My kids rushed up the aisle, snatching up highlighters, pens, and colorful notebooks. My son grinned as he dropped an armload into the cart.

"Can I get a big box of crayons? Can I, Dad?" my daughter asked. She held up a box that claimed it held two hundred and fifty different colors.

I nodded, distractedly. My focus was on a big display of decorative duct tape.

Pink.

Rainbow.

Mermaid scales.

Dinosaur patterned.

I tossed the dino one into our cart. It'd be fun to use during my kidnappings.

31

They Didn't Know

Everyone thought it was fake, our Halloween House. They all paid ten bucks to get in. Hundreds of people came to see it.

They thought it was fake. So they loved it. All the blood, gore, and madness.

They laughed in disgust at the man who took a bath in human blood.

They cheered when the scientist performed painful experiments on humans subjects.

They squealed with delighted terror as the woman cut chunks off a screaming man and ate them in front of him.

They laughed at the woman covered in spiders.

They didn't know the truth.

So they laughed.

32

Boyfriends and Background Checks

I have a new boyfriend. He's great. He's funny and super hot. Great in bed. Recently, one of my friends suggested I run a background check on him.

"You can't be too careful!" she said as we sipped coffee together.

I nodded and promised her I would think about it.

She does know that I already checked up on her. I don't want my friend to think I'm creepy.

But I do background checks on everyone. Not just my new boyfriends.

Family.

Coworkers.

Even her.

Everyone.

The world is full of crazies. And she's right. You can't be too careful.

33

In the Shower

I know what you do in the shower. I've been watching you for years. I watch all my tenants when they shower.

But you… you're my favorite. I know so much about you. I feel so close to you when I watch you shower.

you shower twice a day.

You sing *Disney* sounds at the top of your lungs.

You hate shaving.

You use strawberry shampoo.

You write swear words on the glass.

I wonder what you would do if you knew I was watching? Would you be mad? Or would you be flattered by how much I like you?

34

Texts and Bleach

My phone buzzed. I flinched and glanced at it. The only person who ever called or texted me was Mom. And I couldn't ignore her.

Slowly, I picked up the phone and checked it.

There was a simple, three-word text.

Come help clean.

Great.

She'd made a mess again.

Reluctantly, I went to the basement. Mom was already there, scrubbing at a bloodstain. "Get more bleach. This idiot bled a lot."

"Right," I stepped over the limp body.

"Hurry! You know, we can't leave evidence."

I checked the cupboard. "There's not enough," I whispered.

"Then go get more!" Mom ordered.

35

Eva Wonders

Eva really liked her new job at the gas station. She grinned when her classmate Jordan came in.

He waved at her and made a beeline for the coolers.

"Are you okay?" she asked as she rang up six different energy drinks. He looked even more tired and twitchy than usual. And that was saying something.

Jordan nodded, avoiding her eyes. "Just been helping Mom clean. Had to get more bleach."

"Ew," she laughed sympathetically.

It wasn't until he was gone that she saw the reddish stains his sneakers left behind. It looked like…

Blood?!

What exactly were they cleaning?

36

Waiting

When will you be home? I text my son. He's so *slow*. He *knows* I'm in a hurry.

I'll need to punish him. To remind him how important speed is in these kinds of situations.

I glare at the dead body. It's sprawled across the floor. Now that all the life was gone from it, it'd lost its appeal.

Now it was just a mess to clean up and get rid of.

My phone beeps. It's Jordan.

Almost home. Had to get energy drinks.

Yep. He'd be punished. No one kept me waiting like this. Especially not for energy drinks.

37

Why Some Kill

Some kill for revenge. To get even.

Some kill for justice. To make sure people pay for their crimes.

Some kill for self-defense. They'll only kill if it's the only way to stay alive.

Not me.

I don't kill for those sorts of things.

I kill because I like it.

Love it.

The fight they put up. The screams they make. The light leaving their eyes. That's my favorite part. The light in their eyes going out. The thing that makes them *them* leaving their bodies.

It's intoxicating, having that kind of power over another person.

That's why I kill.

38

The Deadly Couple

They've been all over the country. They've killed people in nearly twenty states. The police are desperate to find them, but they're always one step ahead of them. It's a couple, the police and newspeople say. A young man and woman.

They lure people away into dark alleys and kill them.

Then they flee to the next state and start again.

They're one of the most deadly couples in history, they say.

I've seen the surveillance footage of the man. I know him. I used to date him.

Now all I can think is how that could have been me.

39

Books

His family thought he was weird. That his passion for true crime was just a phase. He was a teen, after all. He probably just wanted to look edgy.

"He'll grow out of it soon," his parents said.

His friends thought he wanted to become a criminal psychologist. They thought he wanted to study the people in the books. "He's gonna be on those crime shows someday," his friends said.

They were all wrong.

He wasn't reading them because he wanted to study the killers.

No.

No, he read the true crime books because he wanted to be those killers.

40

Pay for the Sketchy Shit

I know why people come here. It's a shitty motel, so of *course*, people don't come here for a relaxing getaway. They come here for sketchy shit.

People come here for hookers. People come here for cheating on their partners. People come here for drugs.

People come here with people who don't want to be here. People come here to sell other people.

And people come here to kill other people.

And honestly?

I don't care what anybody does here. Do whatever you want as long as you pay for the damn room, okay?

Just pay me, and we're good.

41

Too Pretty

I had to kill her. She was so pretty, our neighbor.

Too pretty.

What if my husband started to want her?! I had to make sure that he wasn't tempted away from me. I had to.

I was helping him stay faithful to his marriage vows. I was being a good wife.

She was too pretty! Don't you understand?!

This was the only way.

Come to think of it, the woman up the street has really nice hair and legs. Maybe I should get rid of her too. To keep my dear husband faithful.

You know, because I love him.

42

Running Out

I sorted sadly through the last of our food. Rice, beans, and two dusty cans of peaches. There was only about two more days worth of food left. And when it ran out... I didn't know what we were going to do.

My stomach rumbled as I put my share of the food back. My children had to eat. So I would go hungry.

The food was almost gone. The money was *very* gone. Even the water was running out. My children didn't know things were so dire. And no matter how bad things got, I hoped they never would.

43

Free to Go Out

I wait for them to go to sleep. Then I kill them.

One.

By.

One.

I go after the weakest first. I smother my son. I use a pillow. It's easy. Then I kill my daughter. I strangle her. It's a little harder to kill her, but I manage.

Then, I go to the master bedroom. My husband dies with a cheese knife in his gut. He's the hardest to kill. Not because I like him or anything sappy like that. But because he fights back hardest.

When they're all dead, I smile.

I'm free.

I can finally go out.

44

How Long?

I know I shouldn't do it. But it's the one thing that makes me... anything. The rest of the time I just feel numb.

Maybe it's excitement? This thing I'm feeling?

I don't really know anymore. I just know it's *something*.

And I have to keep doing it.

What am I doing, you ask?

Stealing.

I guess it's not the worst thing a person could do. I mean, it's not as bad as murder. And I'm not taking anything important. Just little things. Candy, toys, or crayons.

But I do wonder... how long do I have before it stops working?

45

Can't Let You Live

"You don't have to do this!"

"Oh, but I do."

"Please! Just let me go!"

"I can't do that. I know you'll just run straight to the police."

"No! No, I won't say anything! I promise!"

"I can't believe that. You saw my trophies. You know I killed them"

"I won't tell! I won't go to the police. I'll leave town! I'll never come back!"

"I can't risk it."

"Don't do it! Please don't!"

"I have to."

"Ronda! Put the gun down. Ronda, please! Put it down!"

"I'm sorry. I do like you… I just can't let you live."

Bang!

46

I Love Science

I love science.

It started with those cute science fairs we had in school. Then it grew from there.

My experiments went from innocent titles like, "Do plants grow better when they listen to classical music?" and "Does mold grown faster on white bread or wheat bread?"

To "How much bleach can I inject in a person's veins before they die?" and "What is the loudest a person can scream?"

But by far my favorite science experiment has been: "How many tapeworms can a person have inside them?"

That was so gross and fun.

Did I mention I love science?

47

The Perfect One

I drive around the city for hours, looking for just the right person. They have to be perfect. Otherwise, it won't be fun to kill them.

One man is too tall. So he gets to live.

One woman is too round. She gets to live.

Three different teens are too ugly, so they get to live.

As the night gets later and late, I worry that I won't find anyone.

And then…

I spot him.

The perfect one.

He sits alone at the bus stop, nose in a book.

Good.

I like sneaking up on my prey and surprising them.

<h1 style="text-align:center">48</h1>

Sodas and Popcorn

First, she makes sure no one is looking. Then she takes the bottles of sodas out of her bag. They look exactly like the ones on the store shelf.

But these are filled with poison. Horribly painful, fast-acting poison.

She quickly mixes them to the display, so there's no way to tell the poisoned ones from the safe ones.

Humming to herself, she goes on about her shopping like she hasn't just done something terrible.

She buys popcorn for her after-dinner snack. It will be so much fun to watch the news tonight. She always wanted to do something TV-worthy.

Favorite Colors

Everyone at school thought I was weird. But this morning real sealed the deal for me.

Our new English teacher asked the class to say our names and favorite colors. And to say why it was our favorite color.

Like always, the popular kids went first.

Fred liked blue and white because they're our school colors.

Mary liked green because it's the color of money.

Brian liked brown because his favorite food is chocolate.

Then It was my turn. And everyone freaked out. I said I liked purple because it's the color of a human spleen.

Should I have lied?

50

Sins of the Parents

Our daughter didn't look right.

The priests told me and my husband she was demonic. That we had to get rid of her. I didn't want to.

This wasn't her fault. It was our fault. We must've sinned terribly for God to punish us so, the priests said.

I didn't believe them, but one woman can't fight the church.

They said we had to abandon her, or face exile from the village. So we did, even though it nearly killed me. We left her in the woods to die.

Alone.

Frightened.

I didn't sin before, but I certainly did tonight.

III

The Ghastly Ghosts

51

Wrong

Ghosts aren't real.

I hate when people say that. You wouldn't be so quick to dismiss them if you could see what I see.

The dark shadows that follow you. The evil, grinning faces that leer at us all in bathroom mirrors. The tall, grey, soulless things that stroke your hair at night.

There's nothing after death.

People are wrong about that too. There is something after we die. Something dark, endless, and horrible. Something filled with pain and demonic monsters you could never fathom.

I wish I was wrong.

But I know where we're going.

And it's not Heaven.

52

In the Mirror

I weigh myself just like I do every Friday morning. I groan and resist the urge to break my scale. How could I have gained weight again?! Frustrated tears fill my eyes, but I won't let them fall.

"Oh, please don't be sad!"

I squeal and spin. I live alone, so who was talking?

"In here," the voice says.

Tap.

Tap.

Tap.

That sound…

It's coming from the mirror.

Slowly, so slowly, I turn to look.

My reflection looks dead and decayed. Her eyes are as dark as night. It grins at me. "I think you look great," It whispers.

53

My Second Shadow

It's been following me ever since I came back from the haunted forest.

My second shadow.

It mirrors my first one. But every day, it grows tall, its limbs longer, its head bigger.

No one else has noticed it yet. Maybe no one else can see it.

But I know its real.

I just don't know how to get rid of it.

I peek at it as I walk home from work. It smacks and kicks at my original shadow, clearly laughing at its pain.

Laughing at *my* pain.

I muffle my sobs. I'll have bruises when I get home.

54

The Ghost and the Clothes

"Why don't you ever hang your clothes up?" My roommate asks. We're on my bed, playing video games. "Your closet's huge!"

I pretend to be hyperfocused on the game. "Just lazy, I guess."

"But your clothes would have fewer wrinkles!"

"I'm not trying to impress anyone." My laugh sounds forced.

How could I even begin to explain that the day we moved in, I saw the previous owner?

He hung by his neck in the closet. He's *still* hanging there. I can't put my clothes in there. He doesn't like it.

I know better than to make a ghost mad.

55

Those Things

I am *not* scared of the dark. I'm twenty-seven freaking years old. I'm much too old to be scared of something like the dark.

I am, however, terrified of the things that live *in* the dark. Those… those are *much* more terrifying. Those are the things you have to worry about.

The cold, laughing things that want me to join them. The things with dead eyes.

Those things are why I refused to get out of bed at night. Even when I have to go to the bathroom.

Those things keep me up at night.

Those things, I'm scared of.

The Dripping

Drip.

Drip.

Drip.

It's an awful, constant noise, the dripping.

Drip.

Drip.

Drip.

I checked every sink and tub in the house. I checked each room's ceiling. But I didn't find anything. No leaks, no broken taps.

But still. Something *had* to be making that sound.

Drip.

Drip.

Drip.

It sounded like the noise was following me from room to room. How was that possible?!

Drip.

Drip.

I swallowed. Silence was worse than drips.

A slimy, and invisible hand gripped mine.

"Come swim with me," a voice whispered as the invisible hand pulled me towards the backyard.

And the pool.

Something's in the Chair

He was proud of himself. He just did his laundry for the first time in forever. It smelled so fresh and clean. He deserved a soda for this. Now he just needed to fold it all and put it away.

He dumped the clean clothes out onto his armchair and went to the fridge.

He frowned over the top of his root beer can at the pile of clothes. It didn't look right. Almost like it wasn't on the chair. Like it was piled on someone.

The pile moved, clothes falling everywhere. A shadowy shape rose and moved towards him.

58

The Lonely Ghost

I felt so bad for him. He must've been terribly lonely. I know I'd be, if I was trapped under a house for thirty years.

So I started visiting him.

Nothing crazy, just sitting by the crawlspace under the porch and chatting with him about my days at work.

The ghost liked the company. He started leaving me little notes in the mornings, scratched into the deck.

Hello.

Friend.

Friends forever!

It was cute. Until late one night, he crept from the crawlspace. And made his messages into promises.

"Friends Forever!" He hissed as he dragged me into the crawlspace.

59

In the Bathroom

It happens every midnight on the dot. My bathroom door slams. The lock click. Someone sobs and pleads behind the door, even though I know no human is there.

Then the dark, shapeless mass shoots across my bedroom. It crawls up the door and surrounds the knob. Then the doorknob rattles, like the mass is desperate to get inside.

Then the pounding starts.

Bang!

Bang!

Bang!

It beats on the wood.

The sobbing inside intensifies. "Please! Leave me alone!"

Then the door opens. The sobs become screams.

It's horrible, but what can I do?

How can you help a ghost?

60

The Supernatural Section

It's horrible and fascinating at the same time. I can't look away.

The ghost floats by a wall, silver and see-through in the dimness of its graveyard enclosure. Its body is skeletal. Its ears are missing. The eyes too.

Dark silver drips down and vanishes before it hits the floor.

Blood.

I grimace.

I know people have to suffer horrible deaths to become ghosts, but this is a bit *too* horrible.

My boyfriend squeezes my hand to get my attention. "Want to go see the penguins?"

I smile and nod, happy to be leaving the supernatural section of the zoo.

61

The Book and the Dare

How to Summon Ghosts.

That's the title of the book I need.

But you have to be eighteen or older to buy dark magic books.

I'm twelve.

I should go look at the kids' books. I should put this back.

And I do.

I *do* go back to the kids' section of the bookstore. But not before slipping the ghost summoning book into my backpack.

I know it's wrong to steal. I know summoning ghosts is super dangerous.

But I have to do it. My friends dared me to summon an evil spirit. And I never turn down a dare.

62

The Ghost-in-Law

My mother was a horrible person in life, and she's a monster in death.

Literally.

She died last week. Her body is gone. It's buried deep in the ground of the local cemetery.

Her body is gone.

But her spirit isn't.

She's still around. Judging me. Torturing me. Letting me know all about it when she thinks I've screwed up.

Like today. She took all the dishes out of the cabinets and stacked them in a pyramid on the kitchen table. Even left me a nasty note carved into the tabletop.

Not clean enough. Do it again, you lazy pig.

63

The Stealer Ghost

I like haunting this family. They're very forgetful, very disorganized. I can steal almost anything I like from them, and they don't notice.

I steal lots of stuff I like and hide it with my body under the basement stairs.

Shiny coins. My grandma gave me spare change when I got to visit her.

The toys from fast food kids meals. I always liked those.

And I steal knives.

I don't take those because I like them. I hate them.

I just don't want this family's kids to die the same way I did.

Stabbed.

Scared.

Crying.

Covered in blood.

64

In the Hall Closet

I'm playing hide and seek with my little cousin. She's seeking. I'm hiding.

She tried to tell me I wasn't allowed to hide in the hall closet.

"It's the rule," she said. "The landlord said we can't use it at all."

Which meant that I had to. I wasn't gonna let her tell me what to do.

I shut myself inside.

It was dark.

Cramped.

Dusty.

I smothered a sneeze as my cousin shouted, "Ready or not, here I come!"

"And here I am," a voice whispered as cold hands wrapped around my throat, cutting off my screams of fright.

65

Midnight Mother

I cover my ears as the clock strikes midnight.

It's loud, our old grandfather clock. But that's not why I cover my ears.

I cover my ears so I don't hear my mother screaming.

Even though she's been gone for three years, I still hear her dying moments.

Every night, at midnight.

Her running footsteps.

Her body hitting the wall.

Her pleas. "No! Josh, don't!"

The sound of the baseball bat smacking her.

Her wails of pain among the cracks of bones breaking.

I sob into my pillow. When I prayed to have her back, this wasn't what I meant.

66

The Worst the Ever

I used to think dying was the worst thing that could happen to a person.

I was wrong.

It's not dying.

No.

The worst thing that can happen to a person isn't dying.

It's becoming a ghost.

It's watching your family go on without you. Watching them die and go to Heaven while you're stuck.

It's a special kind of lonesomeness and misery that not even haunting can fix.

You're trapped.

You're alone.

And it's *forever*.

And you're *dead*, so there's no way to escape it. You just go on forever, slowly becoming angrier and angrier.

Slowly becoming a monster.

The Death Game

"This is supposed to be fun?"

"Yes!"

"Really?"

"Yes!"

"Can't we just play Candyland?"

"No! We have to play the death game!"

"So… what do I do?"

"Go in the bathroom with the candle. Keep the lights off. Chant, 'come kill me, demon!' Then blow out the candle and turn on the lights."

"And it'll be right behind me?"

"Yeah!"

"That's fun?"

"Yes!"

I roll my eyes, but light the candle and step into the bathroom.

I chant the words. I turn on the lights.

I scream. There's a demon behind me. I try to run.

But it's too late.

68

The Last Man

The father was the last one.

Literally, the last man standing.

The rest of his family was dead at his feet. Killed by his hands, but not his mind.

That was all me. I took him over so I could enjoy the feeling of killing again. It was nice. I loved the feel of their blood on my hands. Well, the father's hands.

Whatever.

The point was, they were all dead.

The daughters.

The cousin.

The wife.

Now, all that was left was to kill the father.

I laugh.

I take over his body and lead him to the window.

69

The Dead People

My daughter's artwork is starting to scare me. She no longer draws cute little flowers or happy unicorns.

Now, all her drawings are of dead people. Bloody, mutilated people with horrible, painful injuries.

People I had killed.

But how could she know about my victims? They were all long gone, rotting in shallow graves in the woods.

My daughter smiles as she shows me her latest drawing. A boy drowning in a bucket full of his mother's blood.

"Why did you draw this?"

"They wanted me to!"

"Who?"

"The sad people. They want you to know they're waiting for you."

70

The Man in the Fire

I watch the fire crackle, thrilled for it to finally be Fall. I hate the summer, so I'm always super excited when the weather gets chilly enough to have fires.

It's bright and cheerful. It makes such a beautiful orange glow across the living room walls.

Suddenly, the fire goes out.

I stare at the smoking logs in confusion. That's impossible, for a roaring fire to go out, just like that.

It roars back to life, but this time the flames are grey and shaped like a person.

A man holding a huge ax.

He steps out of the fire, ax raised.

Something's in the Trunk

I woke up to a flat tire on my car this morning. Thank goodness my neighbor let me borrow his car. I totally owe him some take-out. I sing along with the radio as I drive home.

Thump!

Thump!

Thump!

What was that?

Thump!

Thump!

Thump!

There it was again. Something clunks around in the trunk. I pull into a parking lot and get out to check.

I open the trunk and frown.

It's empty.

At first glance.

Then, out of nowhere, come hands.

Rotting ones that grab me and pull me in.

The trunk lid slams, locking me in.

72

The Red Eyes

They're always watching me. The things with the red eyes. They watch me from every shadow.

From under the bed.

From behind the TV set.

From under the door when I go to the bathroom.

From the darkness of the closet.

From the bottom of the stairs in my basement.

I try to keep my closet closed. That's where most of them stay. They like the darkest, creepies parts of the world.

It's why I avoid going out at night. I don't want those things to get me. I don't know what they are. And I don't wanna find out.

73

In My Sister's Bed

We'd been whispering for several minutes when the door opened and the light clicked on.

"Who ya talkin' to?" My sister scrubbed at her wet hair with a towel and sat on her bed. "What? What's wrong?" she demanded.

I stared at her in horror.

"What?!"

"Y-you were just here! In the bed!" I gasped, clutching my blankets tight around me.

She looked confused. "I was taking a shower."

"But... I was talking to you!"

She shook her head, looking concerned and frightened. "You couldn't have been."

I shivered. If it wasn't her... who had I just been talking to?

74

The House I Haunted

I used to haunt the house I died in. I used to terrorize the families every night until they moved out.

But this family... I don't haunt them. I just watch.

The mother who rules the house with an iron fist is so much more terrifying than anything I could ever do. She hurts them so badly.

Mentally and physically.

Every moment the family spends with her is worst than forever in Hell. Every dream they have is filled with nightmares. Dreams of her, no doubt.

Even I'm scared of her, and I can't be hurt or killed. Not anymore.

Back to My Body

I crawl across the floor, desperate to get back to my body. I know that I'm dead. I know I can't go back.

I keep trying though.

Behind me, the demons growl.

I glance over my shoulder. I wish I hadn't. There are so many of them. inhuman. Their eyes are full of evil.

I crawl faster.

"You… can't go… bbbacckkk…"

I reach for my own hand.

One of the demons grabs my foot. And even though I'm a ghost, it hurts.

They drag me down through the floor. Through miles of rocks and dirt.

Drag me down to Hell.

IV

The Creepy Creatures

76

The Chickens

The chickens cluck, peck, and fight each other as they swarm over the rotting body. It's putrid, stinking.

Absolute disgusting.

But the chickens keep fighting. Keep eating. They're skeletal, these dumb bird. But their beady little eyes hold a dark determination to live.

Flies and other bugs scatter as the chickens peel back rotting skin to get the inside bits.

A slimy little bug crawls over my shoes, desperate to escape the mad pecking. But one of the chickens scoops it up, and it's just as dead as the body.

This proves it.

Anything is food when you're hungry enough.

The Ants

When I got lost in the woods and broke my ankle, I knew I was going to die.

I knew it was going to be slow.

Drawn out.

Painful.

I knew animals would eventually come to eat my dead body.

But I didn't know they'd start when I was still alive. And I never thought the first things to start eating me would be ants.

They matched across the ground A neat row of red dots. They tore teeny bits of me away, starting with a small cut.

It got bigger and bigger.

And do did the line of ants.

78

The Witch and the Worm

I can't close my mouth.

I can't fight.

I can't even scream.

I'm completely, utterly, one hundred percent frozen. The witch's spell froze me like this. I can't do anything but lie in silent terror as the worm crawls into my mouth.

It's slick and warm and slimy. It's disgusting.

Worms. My biggest fear since childhood.

I can feel it inching its way over my tongue. I can feel it creeping toward the back of my throat.

It slithers down, down, down my throat. All three feet of it, until it's settled happily in my stomach with all its friends.

Ticks

Everyone likes pets. Some people like dogs. Others like fish. My brother has a pet turtle. And my sister has a beautiful parrot. My mom and stepdad are thinking about adopting a cat.

My choice of pets is a little different.

Okay.

A lot different.

My pets are ticks.

Yep. Ticks. Those little blood-sucking bugs.

I like them. I don't know why. I guess they just fascinate me. The way they crawl up anything with their tiny legs. The way they hang onto people and animals so tightly. The way they swell up so huge.

I just think they're neat.

80

Bed Bugs

I was having a nice dream about flying when something woke me up. I lay groggily for a moment, confused. What woke me up?

"Ow!"

Something just bit me!

I jerked back the covers and turned on my phone's flashlight app.

My sheets were crawling with thousands of bugs.

Spiders.

Worms.

Horseflies.

Everything you can think of, it was there.

Oh god!

I jumped up, swearing I slapped desperately at my legs and stomach. Where had these come from?!

As I jumped around, my flashlight jerked around my studio. I froze.

It wasn't just the bed.

There were bugs everywhere.

81

Camping

I didn't want to go camping. (Who went outside in the wilderness for days with no showers or wi-fi for fun?!) But my boyfriend talked me into it.

It wasn't so bad during the daytime. We swam in the lake and cooked hot dogs over a fire.

But then night came.

It was too dark. The ground was too hard. And I couldn't sleep without the drone of Netflix documentaries playing in the background.

But the worst thing?

That would be the animals.

Specifically, the big animal creeping around outside our tent. It kept coming closer.

And it sounded hungry.

82

Locusts

They invaded yesterday. Came in a big dark cloud of buzzing so loud we had to cover our ears as we ran. There must have been billions of them coming at us all at once.

Too many to count.

Too many to stop.

All we could do was run for cover.

When they finally left, and we could come outside again, the gardens were destroyed. Everything nibbled away. Nothing left but twigs.

I felt numb as I stood there, taking in the extent of the damage. It was freaky. Everything… just gone. It would've been impressive if it wasn't terrifying.

The Lost Snake

My day was already bad from waking up late and a shitty shift at work.

Coming home only made it worse. My roommate's snake, Hissy, had escaped her cage again. And he couldn't find her.

"Help me look?" he begged through tears.

I did, though I didn't have much hope. The snake escaped so often. It clearly didn't want to live with us.

We searched the apartment, going slowly from room to room.

We didn't find Hissy. But we did find the little window in the bathroom cracked opened.

"Shit," I muttered. I hoped the neighbors weren't scared of rattlesnakes.

84

The Leopard Seal

It swims round and round my hunk of ice. I want to move. I need to move. But I'm too tired to swim. I lay on my side, panting for air. I can see the shadow in the water every time it passes.

The ice justles, and I flap my wings, desperate to stay on.

The ice jerks again, harder.

Teeth sink into my foot. I'm dragged into the gloom of the water. A face appears in front of me, full of teeth and smugness.

As it finally devours me, I think of my mate and egg. They're doomed too.

Something's in the Kitchen

"Kids! Time for dinner!" I call as I finish setting the table.

They pause their video game, and they come into the kitchen.

"Yay! Chicken!" Luke cheers.

We sit and start eating.

Halfway through dinner, we need more napkins. Jacob goes to get them.

He screams as he opens the cabinet. I rush over. There's something big and hairy attached to his face. I scream too and rip it off him.

The thing flops to the tile and scurries away on eight longs legs, pinchers snapping.

Oh, god.

That thing's loose in the house. And I have no idea where.

<h1 style="text-align:center">86</h1>

<h1 style="text-align:center">The Stranger Sheep</h1>

She fed them every morning, her sheep. She loved them. They were cute and friendly. They greeted her with happy noises and friendly demands for pats.

But today was different.

Today, there were twenty-seven sheep. And it wasn't like they all suddenly had babies either.

There were just… more. This wasn't normal. These new sheep… they were wrong.

They were bad.

Her original sheep ran to her, bleating. These weren't happy bleats though. These were terrified.

Slowly, she opened the gate and let them out. Letting them run loose was better than making them stay in there with the strangers.

The New Pet

When his boyfriend told him he wanted a pet, he was fine with it. Everyone liked pets. He imagined them going to shelters and pet stores together. They would fuss over every little detail until they agreed on the perfect critter to share their home with.

He expected to bring home a dog or cat.

Maybe a tank and some goldfish.

This thing his boyfriend bought…

This wasn't a pet.

This was a monster.

How did he let himself be talked into this? From the safety of the kitchen, he watched his boyfriend enter the cage holding their new tiger.

88

Zombies and Spiders

There's something no one ever thinks about when it comes to the apocalypse.

How do you feed your pets?

I mean, the world is falling apart around me. Zombies run loose. Food is wiped out. It's only a matter of time before the water and electricity are gone.

But what about my pets? They need food.

We're currently in the basement. We're hiding from the zombies. I turn from the window and look at my pets.

I'm almost out of food for them. I try not to cry. I love them. But should I really risk my life for spiders?

89

Truth Dare or Hippo

It was stupid. We shouldn't have done it. I see that now.

we just wanted a great video for our TikTok account. Our fans wanted content, and we couldn't let them down.

So we did the only we could think of.

We started a game of Truth or Dare with them. It was funny at first.

But it got out of hand. Before we knew it, we were breaking into the zoo.

Specifically, into the hippo enclosure.

I never thought they'd be dangerous.

I never thought I'd be in jail.

Or that Chad would be in the morgue.

The Endangered Species

Tigers are almost gone, people say. They're endangered.

But I have some good news.

Tigers will survive.

And when everyone finds out what I've done, I'll be praised across the globe.

Because I've just released three hundred tigers into the wild.

Did you read that right?

Three.

Zero.

Zero.

Three hundred tigers, out in the wild. Sure, they're in the Appalachian Mountains, but my tigers are smart. They'll do just fine out there.

I've been breeding them in secret for years, getting them ready for this. I've even taught them to hunt.

They won't be endangered anymore!

Everyone will be so happy!

91

The Jellyfish

I'm enjoying a quick swim when I bump into them. A swarm of jellyfish.

"Crap!" I whisper in irritation.

One stings me. "OW!" I yell and kick hard in pain. Another one stings too. "Crap! Ow! Ow!"

I try to swim back, away from them.

But it's too late.

And there are too many of them for me to avoid completely

My craps and ows become terrified shrieks of terror and agony as more and more and *more* jellyfish surround me.

Stinging.

Stinging.

Stinging.

My vision goes blurry.

My head slips underwater. Pain takes over.

And the world goes black.

92

The New Hobby

I was so excited when my son finally found a hobby. It was so much better than him just sitting in front of the TV all day. Now he was checking books out from the library, and spending time outside.

Reading and spending time outside.

What more could a parent ask for in an age of internet and social media?

But soon, his hobby started making its way inside. That was less exciting.

The ant farm was okay.

And the crickets were actually kinda cool.

But finding a giant centipede in my bed? On my face?

That wasn't so cool.

93

The First Pet

The lady smiled at me as I cuddled the Yorkie I had just adopted. His fur was so soft.

"I love him already," I grinned. The dog licked my cheek.

"I think he likes you too," the lady said, smiling too.

I thanked her and took my new dog out of the shelter and to my car.

He really was cute. I did like him.

But I couldn't get attached.

Not when Chompy, my alligator was waiting for me at home.

I'd promised him a very special birthday dinner tonight.

And I couldn't disappoint him.

Chompy was my pet first.

94

The Fins

They circle the island I'm stranded on. Like hungry vultures.

If vultures were more than twice as big I was, swam, and had fins that made them look super menacing in the water.

I watch them from the beach.

I'm so hungry.

Thirsty.

And scared.

I'm scared of dying slowly, trapped here with nothing to eat or drink.

I don't want to die like this. Slow and drawn out.

Sure, the sharks will be scary and painful… but at least they'd be quick.

Slowly, I get up.

I walked into the water.

Then I swam.

Right towards those menacing fins.

My Worst Fear

I hate snakes. They're my worst fear.

My family went to a state park for our summer vacation when I was five.

I was bit by a snake.

It was so, so awful.

I almost died.

It's why I don't go hiking. Or even to the park. I like nice urban areas. Places full of people. Areas where the biggest, creepiest wild animals are the occasional rat or a flock of pigeons.

That's why, when my boyfriend asked me on a trip to the beach, I agreed. Beaches didn't have snakes.

No one thought to tell me about sea snakes.

96

The Sting

We're playing in the backyard. My brother digs in the dirt. I'm swinging back and forth on the tire swing. I'm thinking about going inside to get ice cream sandwiches when my brother screams.

I hop off the swing and rush to his side. "What is it? What's wrong?"

My brother clutches his hand and wails. "Get mom!"

"Why? What'd you do?" I couldn't see any blood.

He falls back, scoots away from his dirt pile, and points with the toe of his sneaker.

I take one look at the little brown scorpion and run to find mom.

Her Roaches

She kept finding more of them. Every day, more and more. She should think they're creepy and gross. She should call an exterminator. That was what any normal person would do.

She guessed she wasn't normal, then. Because she liked them. She thought they were kinda cute.

So she started feeding them.

People thought bugs were dumb.

But she knew better. Bugs were smart. Her roaches were smart.

They knew she meant food. They didn't run from her anymore.

In fact, they swarmed around her every time she went to the fridge.

Because they knew: when she ate, they ate.

98

Flies

Flies.

I hate them. They're so small and buzzy and annoying. Constantly crawling all over me and buzzing around my head. I swear that they try and fly in my mouth and nose on purpose. Flies are disgusting like that.

I need to get rid of them. I've tried everything. Sprays. Flypaper. Even just plain, old-fashioned swatters.

Nothing works.

They still find their way into my house. I don't understand why they want in here so bad anyway. I keep everything so neat and clean.

Maybe it's my new friends. They've been really smelly ever since I dug them up.

The New Addition

He hummed his favorite song as he counted his pets' cages.

One for the King Cobra.

One for the Copperhead.

One for the Black Mamba.

One for the Eastern Diamondback Rattlesnake.

One for the Eastern Coral Snake.

One for the Tiger Snake.

And one empty cage on the end for the new snake he was getting tomorrow. An Eyelash Viper. He was so excited, it was going to be a wonderful addition to his collection. Eyelash Vipers were so bright and colorful. He'd spent hours online, looking at photos of them. They were pretty.

He couldn't wait to meet his.

100

The Dangers of Smiles

I smiled at the Chimps at the zoo. I thought I was being friendly.

But the Chimps didn't see it that way.

They saw it as a threat.

They jumped the fence. They tried to kill me. They wanted to. But my husband pushed me out of the way. He got the brunt of the attack. His face was ripped off, his hands torn apart.

I was attacked too, but the chimps were shot before they could hurt me badly.

My husband died. He's my hero. He saved me.

But not my smile.

I haven't smiled since my husband died.

101

Fires and Flashes

After a long day of hiking and exploring, we finally set up the tent and campfire. Well, my wife and I did. The kids played tag.

Once it was all done though, we all relaxed together.

We ate dinner. The kids roasted marshmallows. My wife and I cuddled.

"Selfie time!" My daughter threw her arm around my shoulders and held up the camera to snap a photo.

The flash blinded us. Then we looked at the photo. My heart sped up, terrified by what the flash showed us.

All around us, outside the fire's glow, lurked a pack of wolves.

About the Author

Lennie Grace writes horror short stories and novels and looks forward to sharing her love of all things creepy and spooky with the world. She works two jobs now but someday hopes to write full time.

Lennie loves to write fiction that focuses on dark and creepy things but is extremely nice and non-creepy in real life.

She is a lover of books, reading, and writing. She enjoys reading a little bit of everything, but really likes horror, mysteries & thrillers, fantasy, and manga. Along with reading and writing she also loves animals, coffee, pizza, and all things cute and cuddly.

She lives in Oklahoma in a home filled with books and family members, both human and furry.

You can connect with me on:

https://lenniegracehorrorstories.home.blog

https://www.facebook.com/LenniesHorrorStories

https://www.goodreads.com/author/show/19013373.Lennie_Grace

https://www.amazon.com/Lennie-Grace/e/B07Q3MBFYQ

Also by Lennie Grace

Hello, Readers!

I hope you enjoyed my stories. I had so much fun writing them! If you liked *101 Horror Drabbles*, please, check out my other books. :D

I have lots of different books. From drabbles and flash fiction to full-length novels. :D Here's just a few. To find my complete collection, head over to my Amazon page.

75 Dark and Dreadful Drabbles

75 bite-sized horror stories! All are exactly 100 words long, not including the titles. And all are thoroughly scary! From ghosts and killers, monsters and demons, vampires and dangerous creatures, all kinds of stories reside in these pages!

Some of the stories in this book include:

The Snakes of Justice

A Hell of Spiders

Mindy and the Monster

The Chainsaw Man

The Demon Wife

The Doll's Shadow

Flashes of Fear The Complete Series: A Collection of Flash Fiction Horror Stories

The perfect book to enjoy on Halloween or a dark and stormy night!

This is a truly terrifying collection of tiny stories! Flashes of Fear: The Complete Series! That's right! All 48 original flash fiction stories now available in one book!

Clowns and Chainsaws
The Replacement Brother
What Do Kids Love
Never again

And all the other scary stories! From ghosts and demons, monsters and mad killers, cannibals and clowns, there's something for every kind of horror lover. These stories are all super short. Some are two thousand words. Some are only three sentences long. But all pack a punch! So turn on the lights, grab a blanket, a warm drink, and get ready to enjoy some spooky stories!

This complete series edition also includes some fun extras, you won't find anywhere else! Like:

A list of Lennie Grace's favorite horror stories! Her recommended reading!

And a special sneak peek at Lennie Grace's upcoming novel "Songs For The Music Man."

Tiny Terrors: A Collection of Flash Fiction Horror

Tiny Terrors is a collection of 9 flash fiction pieces. Perfect for readers on the go! Each story is under 1,000 words, making for some super fast, and super creepy reads. There are stories about ghosts, monsters, and human horrors. A little something for everyone.

Includes:

The Pretend Friend

The Hungry Hiker

Can You See Them?

And 6 other spooky little tales. Make sure you read with the lights on!